For Mariam, whose judgment is impeccable, with much love
—L. G.

To my wonderful father in-law, Fred Ashley, for his simultaneous
advocacy of the underrepresented and dedication to the arts
—M. L.

STERLING CHILDREN'S BOOKS
New York

An Imprint of Sterling Publishing Co., Inc.
1166 Avenue of the Americas
New York, NY 10036

ISBN 978-1-4549-3432-5

Distributed in Canada by Sterling Publishing Co., Inc.
c/o Canadian Manda Group, 664 Annette Street
Toronto, Ontario M6S 2C8, Canada
Distributed in the United Kingdom by GMC Distribution Services
Castle Place, 166 High Street, Lewes, East Sussex BN7 1XU, England
Distributed in Australia by NewSouth Books
University of New South Wales, Sydney, NSW 2052, Australia

For information about custom editions, special sales, and premium and corporate purchases,
please contact Sterling Special Sales at 800-805-5489 or specialsales@sterlingpublishing.com.

Manufactured in China

Lot #:
2 4 6 8 10 9 7 5 3 1
06/20

sterlingpublishing.com

Cover and interior design by Irene Vandervoort

Judge Juliette

BY Laura Gehl

ILLUSTRATED BY Mari Lobo

STERLING CHILDREN'S BOOKS
New York

When she was a baby, Juliette's favorite piece of clothing was Mom's old black skirt.

When she was a
toddler, Juliette's
favorite toy was
Grandpa's old mallet.

And when she was in preschool, Juliette's favorite game was settling **cases**.

"Kittykins—you get to be my favorite pet today. Woofster—you get to be my favorite pet tomorrow."

Soon, Judge Juliette was **adjudicating** for the entire neighborhood. "You get half, you get half."

"You lost Kamal's baseball bat; you need to give him a new one."

"You set up your lemonade stand at this end of the street; you set up yours on that end."

"Can I bang the gavel?"

"No, Sergio."

As Judge Juliette's reputation for fairness grew, even grown-ups appeared in her courtroom.

"Yes, Josie should walk the dog before she plays games."

"Eight o'clock is a fair bedtime."

"No, it is not against the law to serve lima beans two nights in a row. It's just mean."

"Can I have a turn with the gavel?"

"No, Sergio."

Outside the courtroom, Juliette was busy pleading her own case with Mom and Dad—the case for getting a pet.

Juliette was not a fan of the answer "Maybe someday," which she did not consider legally binding.

But one night at dinner, Mom and Dad had a surprise for Juliette.
"We think you have become so responsible, with such good
judgment, that you are ready for a pet," Dad said.
"Would you like a dog or a cat?" Mom asked.
"Either one!" Juliette said, hugging both of her parents. "I would
love a dog *or* a cat!"

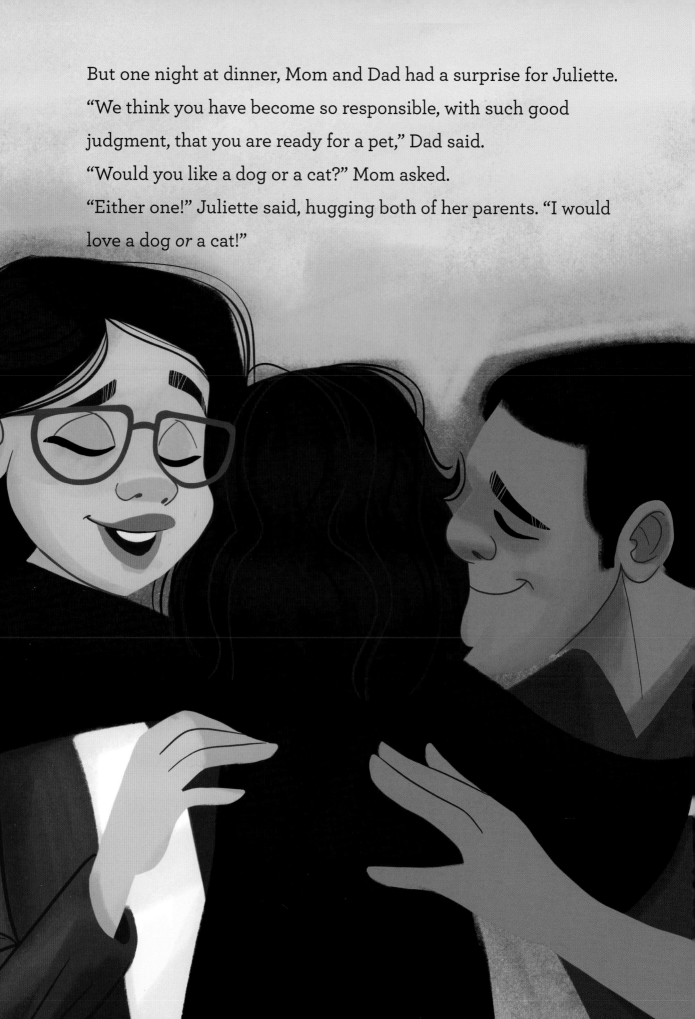

The next day, Judge Juliette had another surprise.
Two people walked into her courtroom, armed with
posters and flow charts.

Mom called **witnesses**.

Dad kept objecting.

Dad walked the court through Exhibit A,

Exhibit B, and Exhibit C.

Mom kept objecting.

"Calls for **speculation!**" "Argumentative!"

Judge Juliette suspected both Dad and Mom were trying to gain an advantage by winning over the spectators.

And Juliette had a distinct feeling that Mom and Dad
were also trying to bribe the judge.

Juliette asked the parties to approach the bench. She tried suggesting a compromise. "Have you considered getting a dog *and* a cat?"

For the first time in days, Mom and Dad were in total agreement:

Judge Juliette did not want to rule on this case.
She hid her gavel.
Mom found it.

She hid her robe.
Dad found it.

She hid herself.

Mom and Dad found her.

Juliette's parents each insisted on making a **closing statement**.

"Ever since I was a little boy, I have wanted a cat . . ."

"When I was a kid, my dog was my very best friend . . ."

But Judge Juliette had her own statement to make.

"I, Judge Juliette, am sorry to say that I must **recuse** myself. Judges are not allowed to rule in cases involving family members."

JUDGE Juliette SERGIO

. . . and a boa constrictor."

legal terms

ADJUDICATING
Adjudicating means making a decision.

CASE
A case is when at least two people, or groups of people, disagree about something, and ask the court to resolve the problem.

CLOSING STATEMENT
At the end of a trial, after all the evidence has been presented, each side gets to give a final speech about why their side is right. This is called the closing statement.

HEARSAY
Hearsay is when a person says something in court that he or she heard somebody else say. Hearsay is not allowed in court.

LEGALLY BINDING
Legally binding means that an agreement, or contract, must be followed. By law, every person who makes the agreement needs to follow its terms.

OBJECTING
Objecting means protesting or disagreeing with what someone says in court.

RECUSE
Sometimes, a judge can't be fair, such as when a case involves members of her own family. In these situations, the judge will recuse herself, or excuse herself as the decision-maker of the case, and ask a different judge to rule.

SPECULATION
Speculation is when a witness gives an answer that is just a guess. This is not allowed in court. Witnesses should only respond to questions if they really know the answers.

WITNESS
A witness is a person who speaks in court about the knowledge he or she has related to a case.

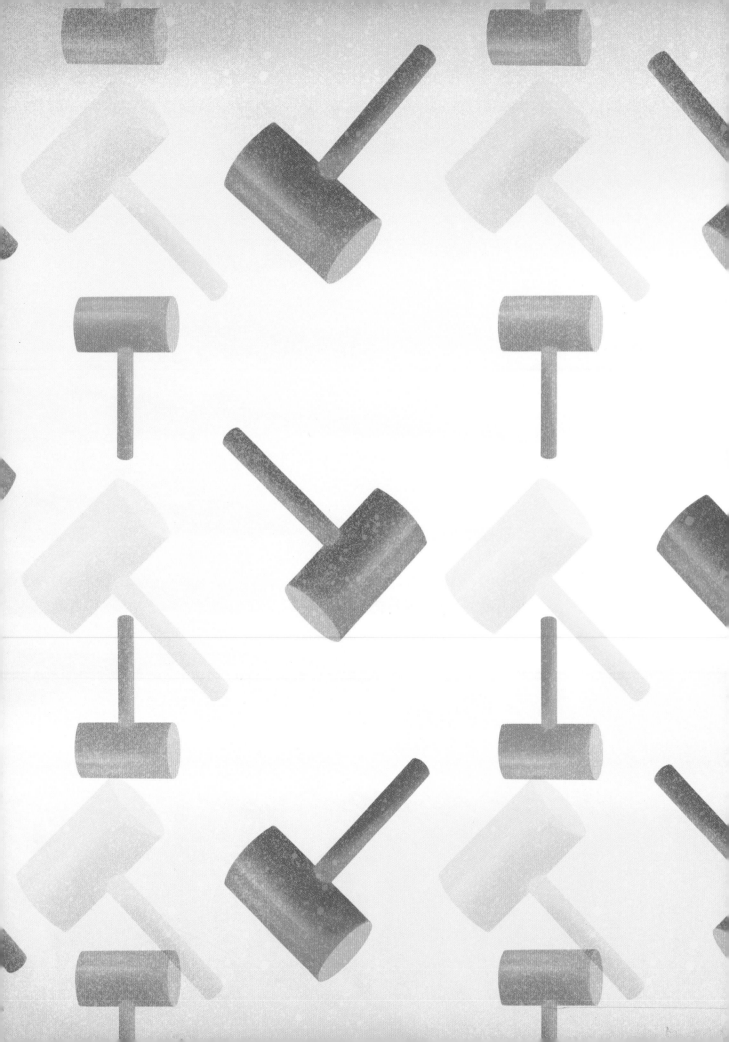